AUSSIE BIG ACHIEVERS

SHANE WARNE

written by RICHARD SIMPKIN

illustrated by DEBRA O'HALLORAN

Other AUSSIE BIG ACHIEVERS books
STEVE IRWIN
CATHY FREEMAN
ASH BARTY

We acknowledge the Traditional Owners of the land on which we publish books, the Quandamooka people, and pay our respects to Elders past, present and emerging.

Published by:
Boolarong Press
38/1631 Wynnum Road
Tingalpa Qld 4173
Australia
www.boolarongpress.com.au

First published 2022

A catalogue record for this book is available from the National Library of Australia

ISBN: 9781922643513 (Paperback)

Printed and bound by Watson Ferguson & Company, Tingalpa, Australia

DEDICATION

This book is dedicated to You,
because You can achieve any dream You have!

AFL

Shane Warne was born on 13 September 1969 in Upper Ferntree Gully, Victoria. As a child, Shane used to enjoy playing various sports including AFL and cricket. Shane's big dream was to play AFL for his favourite team St Kilda.

Though Shane loved AFL, he also enjoyed playing cricket. When he was 14, he was chosen to play in the under-16 Victorian Cricket competition. During this time, most bowlers were fast bowlers, but Shane liked to spin the ball. He had a unique way of making the ball slide, turn and spin at a rapid pace once it hit the ground.

Shane joined the St Kilda Cricket Club, where he was getting noticed as a talented spin bowler. He was also playing AFL, which he loved. Shane played for the St Kilda Football Club under-19 team, and played one game in the reserve team, which was only one level away from being in the senior team. But after two seasons playing for St Kilda under-19s, he didn't make the side the following season.

Shane enjoyed team sports and enjoyed the friendships that you could make while playing with team-mates. Shane knew that, even though he wasn't going to make it as a professional AFL player, he still had dreams of being a great cricket player — he just had to believe in himself.

Shane started to focus on becoming the best bowler that he could. He got noticed as a young cricket player with great potential, and when he was 21, he was asked to join the Australian Institute of Sport Cricket Academy.

On 15 February 1991, Shane played his first game for the Victorian Bushrangers. Shane played just seven matches for the Bushrangers before he was selected to play for the Australian cricket team.

Shane's first game for Australia was on 2 January 1992 against India at the Sydney Cricket Ground. Shane was excited to play for Australia and hoped that he would get a lot of wickets in his first Test match.

Shane's first Test match did not go to plan. After bowling 270 balls, he only got one wicket. In the following Test match in Adelaide, he didn't get any players out. It would have been easy for Shane to just give up, but true champions never do, no matter what! Shane enjoyed speaking to cricket players who had played for Australia before he did, as he felt he could learn a lot about cricket from other champions.

In 1992, Australia was playing against Sri Lanka. Shane had bowled one over earlier in the day, but didn't get anyone out. The Australian captain knew that Shane needed someone to believe in him, so he gave Shane another chance at bowling.

Shane was feeling nervous, but he knew that if there was ever a time that he needed to believe in himself, it was now. Shane took the ball and it spun out of his hand and he took a wicket. All of his team-mates jumped for joy. Shane then took another two wickets, and Australia won the first Test.

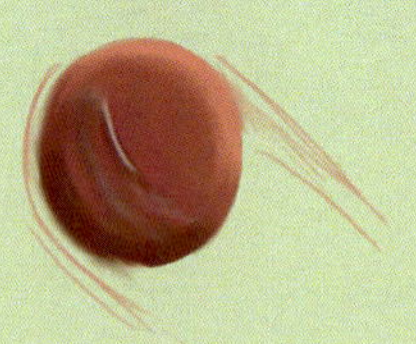

In 1993, Australia went to England to play the Ashes. The Ashes is played every two years between the Australian and England cricket sides. One of Shane's dreams was to play for Australia in an Ashes series. On 4 June 1993, Shane was asked to bowl his first over in the Ashes. With his very first ball, Shane bowled an incredible spin ball and got English batsman Mike Gatting out. The ball was so brilliant that Gatting didn't even see it — it was like Shane was a magician. As time passed, that single ball from Shane became known as *The Ball of the Century*.

During the next Ashes series, Shane took his 150th Test wicket. At the end of the 1990s, Shane was considered one of the greatest cricketers the world had ever seen, and he was named as one of the top five greatest players of the 20th century. The only other Australian in the top five was Sir Donald Bradman. Whether he was playing in Australia or England, New Zealand or India or any other cricketing nation around the world, Shane was breaking records and rewriting the history books.

In the 2001 Ashes series, Shane became the first Australian and the first spin bowler to take 400 Test wickets. He was now focused on becoming the highest Test wicket taker in cricketing history. On 15 October 2004, during the second Test series against India, Shane broke the record for most career wickets in Test cricket by reaching 533 wickets. The following year during the third Ashes match, Shane became the first bowler in history to take 600 Test wickets.

600
test wickets

On 26 December 2006, Shane walked out onto the Melbourne Cricket Ground to the cheers of 89,155 fans. He ran down the pitch and bowled a ball that glided out of his hand. It spun in the air and a second later the stumps fell.

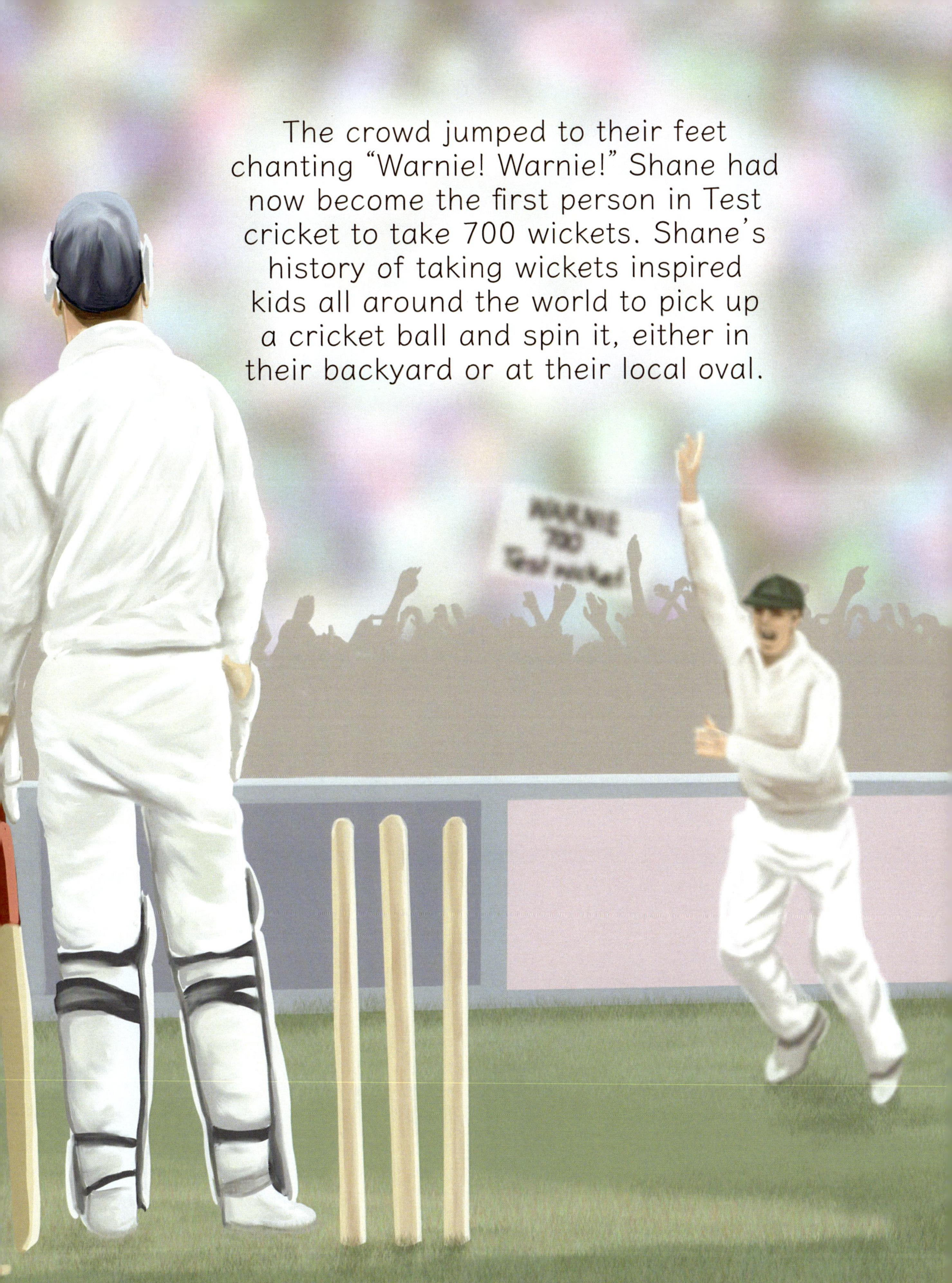

The crowd jumped to their feet chanting "Warnie! Warnie!" Shane had now become the first person in Test cricket to take 700 wickets. Shane's history of taking wickets inspired kids all around the world to pick up a cricket ball and spin it, either in their backyard or at their local oval.

Shane's very last Test match for Australia was at the Sydney Cricket Ground in January 2007. The crowd came to farewell him and say thank you for the magic to their beloved Warnie. On 4 January, during the third day of the final Test match for the Ashes series, Shane bowled his final over.

At the end of the over, the crowd erupted into applause of appreciation. Shane walked over to his adoring fans, took his hat off and bowed to the cheering audience. He retired from Test cricket with a world record of 708 wickets. Not bad for a boy whose first love was AFL.

After retiring from playing cricket, Shane kept himself very busy. He inspired young cricket players to achieve their own dreams. He helped many charities, including The Shane Warne Foundation, which helped sick and underprivileged children in Australia. He also did charity work all around the world.

He was a great dad to his three children, who he adored. Shane proved to us all that, even though you may not succeed at your first dream — in Shane's case, playing AFL for St Kilda Football Club — you can always believe in yourself and achieve many other dreams.

FUN QUESTIONS

[1] What two sports did Shane enjoy playing as a child?

[2] What is the name of Shane's favourite AFL team?

[3] Was Shane known as a fast bowler or a spin bowler?

[4] Where did Shane play his first Test match for Australia?

[5] In 1993, when Shane bowled Mike Gatting out, what did that ball become known as?

[6] Shane was chosen as one of the top five greatest cricket players of the 20th century. Who was the only other Australian in the top five?

[7] What did Shane do that was special on 26 December 2006?

[8] When Shane retired from Test cricket, how many wickets had he taken?

[9] What did The Shane Warne Foundation do?

[10] True or false? If you don't achieve one of your dreams, you can still achieve other dreams that you have.

ABOUT THE AUTHOR

Richard Simpkin was born in Sydney, Australia in 1973 and has worked as a photographer in Australia, England and the US for 25 years.

He is a best-selling author of five books, two of which are about Australian legends who he met, photographed and interviewed.

In 2014 Richard also founded World Letter Writing Day and has inspired children and adults all around the world to take a break from social media and write handwritten letters.

Richard has also conducted many workshops at schools in Australia. The students often ask him about many of the Australian legends that he has met over the years. This has inspired Richard to create these fun yet educational books about iconic Australians who we should all know about.

Other books by author
Australian Legends, 2005
Richard and Famous, 2007
100 Australian Legends, 2014
Michael in Pictures, 2015
Richard Simpkin Celebrity Quotes, 2016
Steve Irwin — Aussie Big Achievers, 2021
Cathy Freeman — Aussie Big Achievers, 2021
Ash Barty — Aussie Big Achievers, 2021

OTHER AUSSIE BIG ACHIEVERS BOOKS

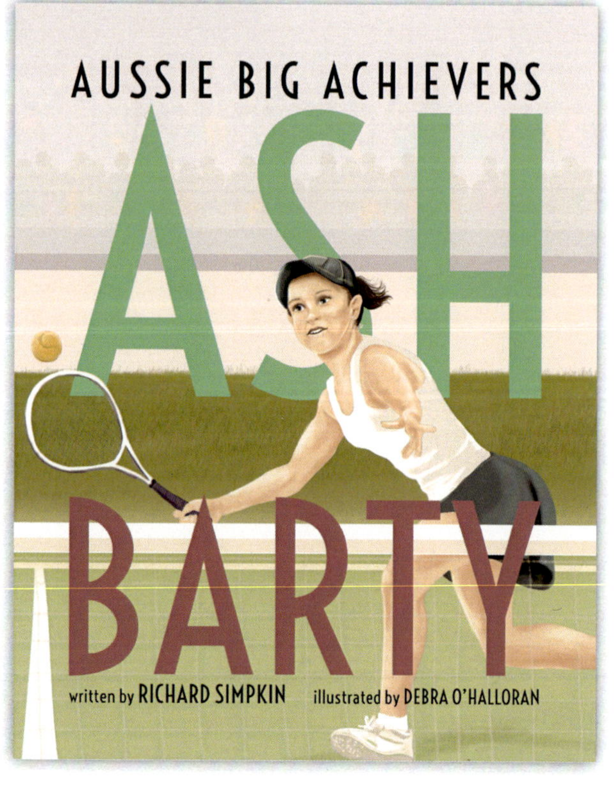